HUBBLE BUBBLE

The GREAT GRANNY CAKE CONTEST!

TRACEY CORDEROY

illustrated by JOE BERGER

nosy crow

An Imprint of Candlewick Press

First U.S. edition 2017

Library of Congress Catalog Card Number pending
ISBN 978-0-7636-9503-3 (hardcover)
ISBN 978-0-7636-8849-3 (paperback)

17 18 19 20 21 22 BVG 10 9 8 7 6 5 4 3 2 1

Printed in Berryville, VA, U.S.A.

This book was typeset in Baskerville MT.
The illustrations were done in ink and colored digitally.

Nosy Crow
an imprint of
Candlewick Press
99 Dover Street
Somerville, Massachusetts 02144

www.nosycrow.com
www.candlewick.com

CONTENTS

The GHOSTS of CREAKINGTON HALL

Chapter One

Splaaaaaaaaat!

A shower of eggs flew across the living room and exploded on the spidery wallpaper. One just missed Pandora's head as she peeked around the curtain, looking for Cobweb, Granny's nervous black cat.

Pandora had been helping Granny do some baking when Granny had decided to test her new magic mixer.

It hadn't minded the butter, or even the bananas, but it hadn't liked kippers, spell books, or socks. So it had exploded, and Cobweb had shot out of the room to hide.

Suddenly, a *booooooooom* could be heard in the kitchen. What had Granny done *now*?

The kitchen was thick with clouds of fluffy flour when Pandora hurried in.

"Granny!" She coughed. "Oh, Granny— are you OK?"

But Araminta Violet Crow was used
to magical mishaps. "Yes, dear!" came
a cheery voice from deep in the swirling
white mist. "I'm tickety-boo! And I'll have
this place shipshape in no time!"

Granny peeked out of the floury fog, and
Pandora giggled. "Oh, Granny," she said.
"You look funny!"

Granny's hat was spattered with egg, and her cloak was dusted with flour. Her favorite frog, Croak, was lapping cake batter off Granny's bent wand.

"I was just making fairy cakes," Granny explained, "when those bad-tempered fairies started throwing the eggs around! Fairy cakes *are* meant to have fairies in them, aren't they?"

Pandora saw three fairies sitting on top of the dresser, scowling.

Granny poked her tongue out at them, and then, with a swish of her wand, began the magical tidy-up. Her supersonic mop scooted around, sending soft, rainbow bubbles into the air. Pink rubber gloves washed her batter-covered bowls. Feather dusters flicked at the dresser, and the three sulky fairies were dusted away—

POP! POP! POP!

"All done!" Granny exclaimed, when the kitchen was sparkling.

"Nearly," said Pandora, pointing at the egg splatters on the living-room wall.

Granny chuckled. "Use your wand, Pip dear. Just magic the mess away!"

Pandora bit her lip nervously. She had something to tell Granny. Something she knew Granny wouldn't like.

Pandora sat Granny down on the sofa and took a deep breath. "I promised Mom I wouldn't do magic," she said. "Not for the entire vacation week."

"Oh, no!" cried Granny. Then she looked thoughtful. "Was it because of what happened at the library?"

Pandora nodded sadly.

Granny and Pandora, in a moment of reckless fun, had magicked the three little pigs out of their fairy-tale book. Then they'd magicked the big bad wolf out, too (to tell him to be nice to the pigs). Trouble was, he was *starving* and the three "little" pigs were actually very fat and juicy and yummy-looking. . . .

The librarian had called Pandora's parents, who were

"very disappointed" in her and
Granny. Now Pandora wasn't
allowed to do magic for a
whole week!

And so when Pandora's mother, Moonbeam, had dropped her off at Granny's house that morning, she'd told her to *"Be good."*

Pandora knew this was really code for *"Keep Granny out of trouble."* But that was easier said than done with a wacky, witchy granny *with a wand*!

Pandora's parents were coming to spend the afternoon with her and Granny. They'd taken time off work specially. But Pandora knew they'd be horrified if all Granny wanted to do was have food fights with fairies!

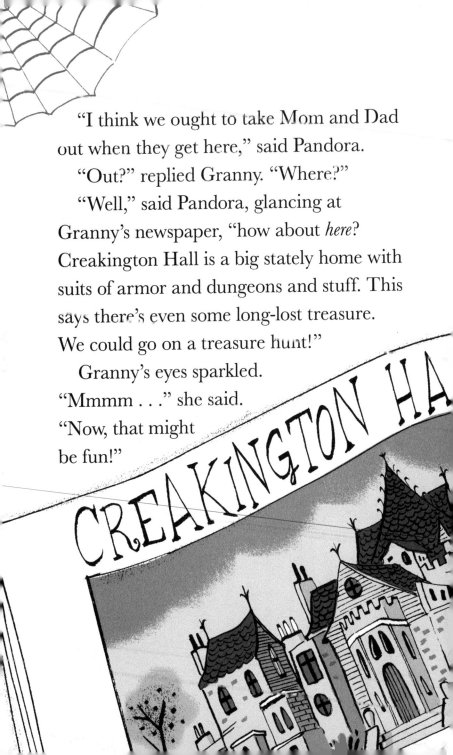

"I think we ought to take Mom and Dad out when they get here," said Pandora.

"Out?" replied Granny. "Where?"

"Well," said Pandora, glancing at Granny's newspaper, "how about *here*? Creakington Hall is a big stately home with suits of armor and dungeons and stuff. This says there's even some long-lost treasure. We could go on a treasure hunt!"

Granny's eyes sparkled. "Mmmm . . ." she said. "Now, that might be fun!"

CREAKINGTON HA

With that, Pandora heard her parents' car pull up outside the house. "Great!" she cried, grabbing Granny's hand. "Let's go!"

Chapter
Two

Granny jumped on her
broomstick.

"Hop on!" she called.
"I can zoom us to Creakington Hall in
a jiffy!"

"No! Not on that!" squeaked Pandora's
mom, Moonbeam (who *could* do magic but
didn't like to).

"Certainly not!" sniffed her dad, Hugo
(who couldn't do magic at all).

With a shrug, Granny reparked the
broom by the pumpkin patch and hopped
into the car. Pandora sat beside her.

"Come on, then!" called Granny. "I
wonder if they have ghosts at Creakington
Hall. I hope so!"

When they arrived, Granny strode into the house swinging her cauldron handbag, which was belching out clouds of green steam.

"Did you really need to bring that?" asked Hugo.

"Oh, yes, dear!" said Granny. "You never know when you'll fancy a nice cup of gloop!"

They got in a short line to buy their tickets. As they waited, Granny's hat gave a sudden wiggle, then a frog peeked out from under it.

R-r-r-ribbit! croaked Croak.
Then he boinged through
the air and landed on
a man's bald head!

Granny whisked out her wand and
magicked him back, but the man's wife
looked puzzled. "I could have sworn you
grew green hair just then, dear."

"*Ridiculous!*" exclaimed her snooty
husband.

Moonbeam and Hugo gulped nervously, but Pandora had to hold in a giggle. Naughty Croak had left a splat of frog poop right on top of the man's shiny bald head!

Pandora gazed around the entrance hall. It looked very run-down, and the place smelled of cabbage and mold.

"Psst, *Granny*!" she whispered. "How about we sneak off on a treasure hunt while Mom and Dad look at all the boring stuff?"

"One of our top-secret missions!" exclaimed Granny. "Oh, yes—I'd *love* to find the treasure!"

"Huh!" came a sneering voice from behind. "Fat chance!"

A freckly boy strode past them, wrinkling his nose at Granny. "If anyone's going to find any treasure, it's me!"

Pandora glared as he marched away. Then things got even worse.

"Let's all take the tour of the house!" cried Moonbeam. "There's so much to see."

Granny and Pandora both sighed. Their top-secret mission to find the treasure had been spoiled.

The tour moved through the house at a snail's pace. Pandora's parents read *every* information card on *every* wall, below *every* painting, beside *every* table and chair. Pandora's dad even took notes!

Granny behaved rather well, apart from loudly yawning every so often and touching things she shouldn't. But Pandora knew that she was getting bored.

And what did Granny *always* do when she got bored? MAGIC!

The tour guide stopped at a portrait of the Fifth Earl of Creakington. He reminded Pandora of a pigeon!

"The earl was a friendly fellow," droned the tour guide. "He —"

"Just winked!" boomed a red-faced woman. It was the freckly boy's mother. "That portrait *just winked*!"

"Ridiculous!" cried the bald-headed man.

"What would *you* know?" said the woman, her cheeks getting redder by the second. "You with the frog poop on your head!"

"POOPYHEAD!" snickered her freckly son.

Pandora looked at Granny, who was giggling behind a pillar. She was up to her old tricks again. Uh-oh . . .

Chapter Three

The tour guide hurried everyone into a
cobwebby dining room. A chandelier hung
from the ceiling, and there were huge
moth-eaten tapestries on the walls. A rusty
suit of armor stood beside the door.

"Hey, *Mom*," Moonbeam hissed. "That
painting back there — did *you* make its eyes
move?"

"Me?" said Granny innocently. "Oh,

look at that *wonderful* vase! Come on, Pandora."

Granny dragged Pandora over to a cracked old jug with a missing handle.

"You can't fool mc, Granny," Pandora whispered. "I know that winking thing was you."

"You're right," Granny admitted with a grin. "But it was just a bit of fun!"

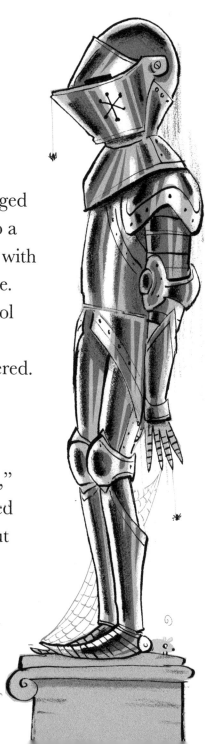

The tour guide pointed to a table that
was laid with a banquet of fake food.
Around it sat mannequins in costumes.
The guide started droning on again, and
Granny edged her wand from her pocket.
Pandora heard a faint WHIZZ! POP!
and gasped.

Suddenly, the fake roast pig on the table BURPED very loudly. Then all the mannequins started to have a food fight!

A roaring fire shot up in the grate, crackling and popping merrily, and the hundred candles in the old chandelier started burning.

"What's happening?" cried the bald-headed man as the rusty suit of armor gave him a squeaky wave.

Pandora saw the freckly boy looking suspiciously at Granny. She felt sure he'd seen her do magic, and now he was going to tell.

Pandora gulped. To keep Granny from getting told off and (shock! horror!) people *staring*, she had to think of something, quick!

"Ghosts!" squealed Pandora in her most excited voice. "Creakington Hall is *haunted*!"

"Ghosts!" Granny laughed,
secretly flicking her wand again.
The rusty suit of armor began
tottering across the room.
As everyone stampeded to the
door in fright, Granny's
pet frog, Croak,
leaped onto her
wand, which sent
spells shooting out
everywhere. . . .
POW! Dusty books flew
off their shelves and started
flapping around like birds.
PING! The piano in the corner began
playing a spooky tune.

BAM! A stuffed deer head on the wall shouted, *"BOO!"* then stuck out its tongue and blew a raspberry!

"Ooopsy!" gulped Granny, putting Croak away.

"Mom!" hissed Moonbeam. "Stop this M-A-G-I-C at once!"

Chapter Four

Granny gave her wand a quick flick, and the magical mayhem stopped.

"Hang on—where's Alfred?" the tour guide said.

"Who's Alfred?" Pandora asked.

"The suit of armor," explained the annoyed guide. He liked Alfred.

"Not to worry!" Granny piped up. "Alfred's probably just gone for a stroll.

And who
could blame him,
cooped up in here
for centuries!
We'll find him!"

They checked upstairs and downstairs, and then they looked in the gardens. No Alfred. The tour guide sighed.

"But we still haven't searched the dungeons," said Granny. "Come on!"

She led the way down the gloomy stairs, the star on her wand shining brightly.

"Aha!" Granny cried as they heard a CLANK . . . CLANK . . . CLANK.

"Alfred!" cried the tour guide with delight as Alfred clattered around the dark, dusty dungeon.

Granny gave her wand a short, sharp flick and the suit of armor froze in mid-clank. But he was standing on only one leg and looked very *wobbly*!

"Oh, no!" Pandora gasped. "Watch out!"

Everybody held their breath while Alfred teetered and rocked. Then . . .

back he tumbled with an enormous
CRASH!

When the dust had cleared, they saw
that Alfred was in pieces. The tour guide
looked furious. It would take ages to put
him back together. Then Pandora gave a
sudden squeal. "Look!"

Inside Alfred's helmet was a dusty velvet
pouch. "Ooooh!" said Granny, her eyes now
bright. She opened the pouch and . . .

"Wow!" gasped Pandora
as a dazzling shower of
diamonds and thick gold coins
rained down onto the floor.

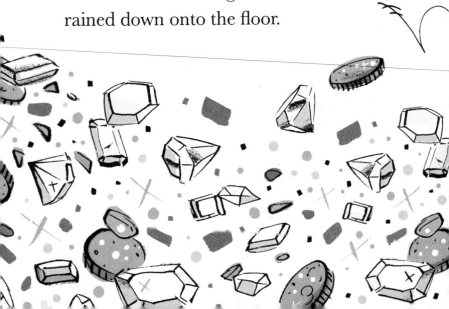

"*Look, everyone—we've found the treasure! Yippee!*"

As a thank-you, all the visitors were treated to a yummy cream cake in the little dining room. The freckly boy scowled at Pandora.

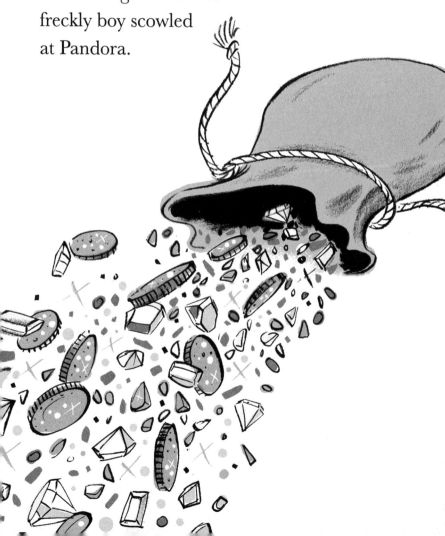

"Huh! If my granny were a witch," he said, "*I'd* have found that treasure first."

Pandora didn't argue, but reached for Granny's wand and gave it a secret little flick. Suddenly, the boy's cake turned into a big slimy toad.

"Ha!" Pandora giggled. "Serves you right!"

The GREAT GRANNY CAKE CONTEST!

Chapter One

"*Goodness!*" cried Granny. "So many cloaks! Which one, Pip dear? Which one?"

Pandora peered into the wardrobe. All of Granny's cloaks were black. "Maybe, um, a *black* one?" she said with a shrug.

Granny took out a long black cloak and threw it around her shoulders. Cobweb the cat gave a nervous *Meeoooow!*

"He says I look like a giant bat!" Granny said, chuckling.

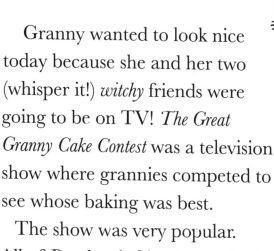

Granny wanted to look nice today because she and her two (whisper it!) *witchy* friends were going to be on TV! *The Great Granny Cake Contest* was a television show where grannies competed to see whose baking was best.

The show was very popular. All of Pandora's friends watched it. So did all of her teachers.

Each granny was allowed to take along one helper. And Granny had chosen Pandora!

Pandora was worried. What if she dropped all the eggs or set the studio on fire? Uh-oh . . .

Granny tied up her cloak. "Time to go!" she said, popping her wand into her pocket.

"But, Granny, there's no magic allowed!" said Pandora.

"I know." Granny nodded. "But I always like to have my wand, just in case!"

When they arrived at the TV station, Granny's friends Gwendolyn and Tilda were already there with their helpers, meanie Merlin and snooty Opal.

The two grannies were having great fun magicking on their makeup. Hairbrushes and lipsticks were flying around all over the place!

Opal and Merlin eyed Pandora as if she were a nasty sea slug. Pandora ignored them, and she and Granny sat down to have their makeup put on.

Pandora *hated* the powder, which made her sneeze and her skin break out in a red spotty rash. "Ow!"

Everyone was then shown into the studio, which had been made to look like a fancy kitchen. The producer told them what they had to do.

"First you will bake your favorite cakes. Then you will make Chef Edwardo's world-famous special dessert. And remember: NO MAGIC ALLOWED!"

"OK!" cried the grannies. It was time. Pandora swallowed hard. She crossed her fingers that all her friends' TVs weren't working today!

Chapter Two

The grannies and their helpers were shown to their tables.

"OK," said the producer. *"Action!"*

Granny had decided to bake butterfly cakes. Pandora weighed out the ingredients and only dropped *one* thing. Unfortunately, it was a huge bag of flour and it exploded all over her.

"Don't worry," said Granny. "It hides your rash *beautifully*, dear!"

As Granny started mixing, Pandora
eyed the others. Tilda was baking a lemon
sponge cake, and Gwendolyn's carrot cake
was well under way. Merlin was a wiz with
the carrot peeler, and Opal was *born* to
squeeze lemons.

Tilda iced her lemon sponge cake with sparkly icing, while Gwendolyn covered her cake with fancy carrot-shaped candies.

Either they had been practicing, thought Pandora, or they baked without magic *a lot,* because their cakes looked very yummy indeed.

Granny's cakes didn't look *nearly* so good. They were rather lopsided and burned around the edges.

"It's OK!" Granny beamed. "I'm not finished yet!"

On the windowsill behind her was a pot of flowers with some butterflies hovering near them.

She opened the window, brought in the pot, and then popped some butterflies onto her cakes.

"Ta-daaaa!" she exclaimed. "What better to have on butterfly cakes than butterflies!"

The judges bustled up, tutting. "*Real* butterflies are not allowed!"

"Oh," said Granny, looking glum.

The judges then awarded their scores. Tilda's lemon sponge cake was the winner, and Gwendolyn's carrot cake came in second. Sadly, Granny's butterfly cakes were disqualified.

Next it was time for the show-stopping special dessert. Chef Edwardo swept in, carrying a platter, and Pandora gulped.

It was a big fancy swan made from swirls of fluffy meringue.

It had wings, a long neck, and a dainty white face. Its eyes were made from licorice circles, and it had two crisp ginger cookies for a beak.

No way could her granny *EVER* make that!

They were doomed.

Granny was having *such* trouble with her
swan. She whisked and whisked the egg
whites, but they refused to make stiff peaks
the way they were supposed to.

"Maybe I should add some glue?" she
suggested.

Pandora shook her head. "You can't put
glue in food, Granny."

Granny sighed.

"Or how about I just use my wand? Just a *teeny* bit of magic, nothing big."

Pandora shook her head again. "No magic!"

Pandora glanced over at the other grannies. Their mixture had LOTS of stiff peaks! Maybe Opal and Merlin were better helpers.

Granny slopped the mixture out of her bowl, and it made a runny puddle on her plate.

"Maybe if we add more sugar?" said Pandora. Granny shrugged.

Pandora headed off to

the pantry but stopped short just outside.
Somebody was already in there. Pandora
peeked around the door and gasped.

Opal was waving her wand over some
eggs and muttering *a magical helping spell:*

"Little eggs, all round and
white, make my granny's
swan so bright!"

Opal was cheating. So *that's* why her granny was doing so well!

Pandora shrank behind the door as Opal dashed back to the kitchen with the eggs and Merlin raced into the pantry.

Pandora watched as Merlin swished his wand over a jar of sugar and commanded it to give *his* granny's swan fine wings. Then he was off back to the kitchen with the jar of magic sugar.

Pandora couldn't believe it. *"How utterly unfair!"* she muttered. Opal *and* Merlin had been cheating all along!

Pandora stomped into the pantry, grabbed a jar of sugar, then thundered back to the kitchen. If *they* could magically help their grannies, *so could she*!

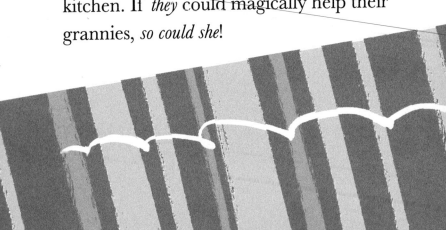

"Sprinkle some of this onto your mixture!" Pandora said to Granny at once.

"But I'm really not sure it will help, dear."

"I am." Pandora nodded. "I'm *very* sure."

Granny sighed. "All right, then," she said, and she started to sprinkle on the sugar.

As she did, Pandora edged Granny's wand out of her pocket and whispered, "Fluffy white wings and a neck so tall— make *my* granny's swan the best one of all!"

68

POOF!

A swirl of magical stars puffed out of the end of the wand. Quickly, Pandora fanned them away. But somebody had seen. . . .

"*Cheat!*" shrieked Opal, pointing at Pandora.

Pandora jumped and, quite by accident, *another* spell burst from the wand. It sent three little eggs zooming through the air, then SPLAT! SPLAT! SPLAT! The eggs landed on Gwendolyn's head. She looked very surprised.

Then a grin spread across her face.

"Oh, goody!" she cried. "Food fight time!"

"Did someone say *food fight*?" Granny asked.

"*Splendid!*" Tilda shouted.

All three grannies grabbed their wands. Then together they uttered the food fight spell:

"SPLATTTIOCIOUS!"

Pandora dived for cover as (take a deep breath) eggs and flour and sugar and lemons and carrots and lopsided cakes and butter and milk and dribbles of sloppy wet swan went flying through the air.

"Stop!" yelled the producer. "STOP!"

Chapter Four

"Arrrgggh!"

The producer slipped on some butter and landed headfirst in Gwendolyn's swan.

"Pffff!" he spluttered.

"Look!" Opal giggled.

"Ha-ha!" Merlin laughed.

And even Pandora snorted.

The producer had wings shooting out of his head, as if he'd grown pixie ears! And the swan's head was sitting on top of his own, like a hat.

Now everyone was covered in egg and flour, but nobody seemed to care. This was *way* more fun than baking any day!

Granny decided to turn Tilda's
meringue swan into a *real* one, just for fun.
But it turned out to be *really* grumpy.

When the producer tried to catch it, the
swan started nipping his bottom.

NIP!
NIP-NIP!
NIP!
NIP!

"Noooo!"
he cried.

The Great Granny Cake Contest had finished. No one had won, but none of the grannies cared.

With a swish of their wands, they cleaned up the mess. They were starting to feel a bit sorry for the producer, but he'd disappeared.

"Maybe he's still being chased by that swan," said Pandora.

It was time to go home. But just as they were about

to zoom off on their broomsticks, the producer suddenly showed up. Pandora could see a bit of cookie-beak left on the top of his head.

"Oh, hello, dear!" chimed the grannies.

"Sorry about the swan," said Pandora.

"Never mind about that!" The producer was smiling. "Hundreds of viewers have called in to say they really loved the show! So how about, well—doing MORE? *The Great Granny Knit-a-Thon, The Great Granny Shopping Showdown*—a new thing every time!"

"With magic?" asked Granny.

"Definitely!" the producer cried.

All three grannies agreed at once. It was going to be a hoot! Then they all zoomed off home for tea.

"Shall I bake us a pie, dear?" Granny asked as they flew over the town.

But Pandora had had enough *baking*! "What about fish and chips?" she said.

So that's just what they had. They stopped in the park and ate them by the pond.

"When I do these shows," said Granny, "I shall need a little *helper,* you know."

Pandora nearly choked on a fry.

Uh-oh . . .

ALAKAZOOM!
The BIG BUNNY
BOOM!

Chapter One

"Dead," Nellie said, lifting up a limp carrot stalk.

"We'll lose the gardening competition," Clover said with a sigh.

"No, we won't," said Pandora. "My carrots are just a bit droopy, that's all!"

Pandora and her friends were at their after-school gardening club. It was run by Pandora's granny, a wacky (whisper it!) *witch*.

For weeks the club had been growing fruits and vegetables for a big competition that was being judged the next day.

The prize was a school trip to Beanstalk Land, a super-cool farm with an adventure playground in the shape of a giant beanstalk.

Pandora sighed and plodded off to tell Granny about the droopy carrots.

After she had waited a bit in the cobwebby garden shed, Granny swept in. She was carrying a tray of pansies that all seemed to have grown little faces!

"Um, Granny," Pandora said, "have you *done* anything to those flowers?"

"Like what?" Granny grinned, quickly slipping her wand back into her cloak pocket. The pansies poked out their tongues at Pandora and giggled.

"Granny," said Pandora, "my carrots are looking a tiny bit . . . ill."

"Not anymore!" Granny smiled. "I just whizzed them up a drink, and now they're fine!"

"Really?" Pandora smiled. "Thanks a lot!"

But suddenly she remembered Peter, Granny's prize pumpkin. Once Granny had whizzed Peter up a get-well drink. It had been a fizzy pink *growing potion*. Five minutes later, Peter was the size of a gorilla!

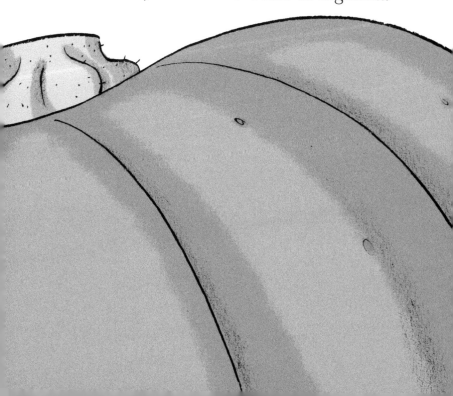

"Eeek!" squeaked Pandora, jumping
to her feet. "Was the drink you gave my
carrots, sort of . . . pink?"

"Err . . ." muttered Granny. "Oh, golly—
is it time to go home *already*?"

Granny dashed outside and grabbed her
broomstick, and they both climbed on.

Pandora still looked worried as she put on
her helmet.

"But, Granny, using magic is —"

"Got your lunch box?" Granny asked.

"Yes, but —"

"*Good!* And your reading book?"

"Yes," said Pandora. "But what about my *carrots*?"

"Off we go!" said Granny. "Hold on tight!"

As they whizzed home through the fluffy clouds, Pandora was still thinking about her carrots.

What if Granny *had* fed them fizzy pink potion? Yikes!

Chapter
Two

The next morning, Granny whooshed
down Pandora's chimney.

"Mom," Pandora's mother said with a
sigh. "You really should use the door."

"We might have lit a fire!" Pandora's dad
scolded her.

"Oh, Granny—you're all sooty!"
Pandora giggled.

Granny cleaned her sooty clothes with a
flick of her wand. Then they all sat down

to breakfast. Granny magicked up a jar of beetle-currant jam and spread a thick black dollop on her toast. She took a big bite, and Pandora shuddered.

"Mmmm." Granny smiled, licking her lips. *"Delicious!"*

After breakfast, Pandora's parents left for work and Pandora told Granny about Plop.

Plop had been the class goldfish. But last week he'd died. Plop had never done much except swim (and plop), but he'd been very nice all the same.

"Oh, that's too bad, dear," said Granny.
"So do you need a new class pet?"

She wiggled her wand and a shower of
stars shot out of the end. BANG!

Pandora peered through the starry smoke

and saw a cute baby dragon on the rug. "Ta-da!" exclaimed Granny.

The baby dragon gave a little hiccup, and giant flames shot out of his nostrils.

"But, Granny,"
gasped Pandora,
"my teacher won't
let us have a *dragon*."

Grumbling, Granny made the dragon vanish, then put out all the fires he had started. Luckily her wand made a very good hose!

"Right," said Granny finally. "Time to go to school!"

It was going to be a very big day. Granny had lots of flowers to plant before the judges arrived. She wanted to make Pandora's school look perfect.

When they got there, the playground was packed with shouting children. Granny's gardening club raced over to Pandora.

"We're going to win today!" Jake cried.

"Yes!" agreed Nellie. "Come and see your carrots!"

Bluebell opened the garden gate, and they whisked Pandora inside.

They passed Jake's nice
firm runner beans.

They passed Bluebell's rows of potatoes.

They passed Nellie's strawberries and
Clover's raspberries, all looking lovely and
juicy.

Finally, they came to the carrot patch. Pandora stopped and gasped.

"OH, NO!"

Yesterday the carrot tops had been floppy and small, but *now* they looked like giant bushy squirrel tails! And the carrots looked ready to burst out of the ground!

What had Granny *done*? When the
judges saw those carrot tops, they were
bound to say she'd cheated! Then everyone
would (shock! horror!) stare at her!

Chapter Three

Ding-a-ling-a-ling!

The school bell rang, and everyone went in. Except Pandora.

She was rummaging inside her school-bag for her wand and muttering to herself. "I need to magic these carrots smaller, right now!"

Then she remembered that she'd used her wand to magic her teeth clean that

morning. She must have left it on the
bathroom sink. "Oh, no!"

Sighing, Pandora plodded into the
classroom and plonked herself down next
to Nellie.

First there was a math test. Then they all
wrote a story. But poor Pandora couldn't
stop thinking about *carrots.* . . .

Pandora's teacher marked their tests.

"Pandora Isabella Podmore!" he scolded

her, waving her
book in the air.
"Nineteen minus
eight does *not*
equal carrot!"

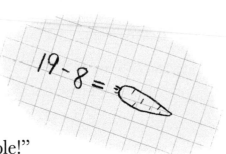

"Sorry, Mr. Bibble!"
said Pandora.

"And," he added, holding her story,
"you were meant to write about the *Romans,*
not *carrots!"*

"And look!" Bluebell giggled. "She's
drawn a *carrot* instead of a *chariot!"*

After lunch, it was finally time for the
judging of the gardening competition.

Pandora's knees knocked as Mr. Grimly,
the principal, brought in the three judges.
One of them was tall and skinny and
looked like a runner bean. Another wore
a thick brown suit, as hairy as a coconut!
The third one was short and round and
reminded Pandora of a turnip.

They walked along the nice clean path,
past the neat flower beds. As they did,
Granny's pansies grinned like Cheshire
cats.

"Such happy specimens!" remarked the
round judge. Granny blushed.

The judges arrived at Jake's runner beans and picked one off. "Hmmm, very good!" said the tall, skinny judge.

Next, Bluebell dug up a few of her potatoes and the judges examined them closely. "Wonderful shape!" the round judge said.

They loved Nellie's strawberries and

Clover's raspberries, too. Then, finally, they came to Pandora's carrots. . . .

"Oh!" said the judge in the hairy brown suit. "What an enormous carrot top!" And he prodded the bushy green leaves with the tip of his pencil.

As he did, the ground beneath the stalk gave a little rumble. Then a whopper of a carrot shot up out of it — POP!

The carrot soared high into the air like a great muddy rocket, showering everyone below in dirt and worms.

"Arggh!" screamed the judges as the giant carrot turned and dropped back down to earth. It crash-landed beside Granny with an enormous thud! Then *all* the massive carrots underground blasted off:

POP!
POP! POP!
POP!

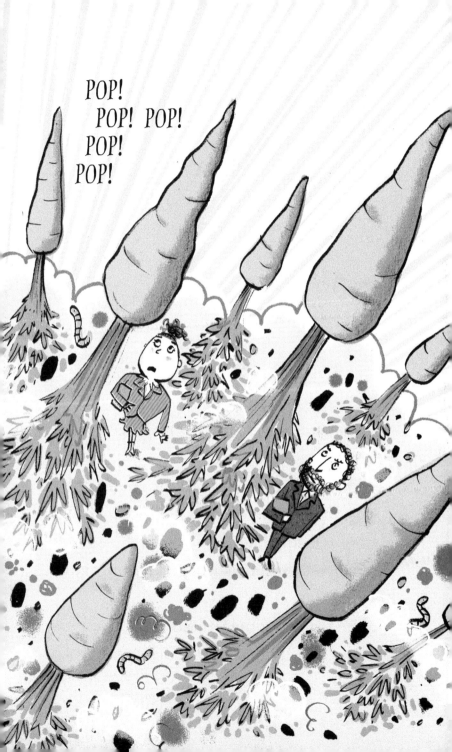

When the downpour of mud and creepy-
crawlies was over, Mr. Grimly looked ready
to explode.

"Disgraceful!" muttered the round judge.
"*Magic* in a gardening competition! This
school is disqualified!"

"But—" Granny shrugged. "I only gave
the carrots a *drink*."

The whole school peered into the
garden, now littered with enormous carrots.

Pandora blushed. "Granny, please make things right!" she whispered.

Granny nodded and whisked her wand from her cloak. Mr. Grimly backed away nervously.

Granny gave her wand a twizzly flick, and a swirl of starry mist shot out. Granny's spell quickly whisked the giant carrots into a tall, neat pile. Then it made the garden shed door spring open — PING!

Three sweeping brooms came dancing
out, followed by some spades and trowels.
Bringing up the rear was a wheelbarrow
filled with bright sunflowers.

As the brooms swept the paths clean,
the spades shoveled soil into the giant holes
made by the exploding carrots.

Finally, the trowels neatly planted the sunflowers where Pandora's carrots had been.

"But," Mr. Grimly spluttered, "what about those giant carrots?"

Granny flicked her wand again. In a puff of smoke, a huge rabbit appeared. "Giant carrots need a giant rabbit to *nibble* them!" Granny declared.

The rabbit bounded over to the carrots and started nibbling like mad.

"He's cute," Nellie cooed.

"He's greedy!" said Bluebell.

"We like him!" chorused Clover and Jake. Pandora liked him, too. Very much!

When the giant rabbit had polished off
the carrots, Granny waved her wand again.
WHIZZ! POP!

Now the rabbit became a teeny-weeny
bunny with the *floppiest* ears, the *fluffiest* tail,
and the *twitchiest* nose in the world!

"Meet your new class pet!" announced
Granny.

"Oh!" cried Pandora. But Granny hadn't
quite finished yet.

Because they'd lost the competition,
there'd be no school trip to Beanstalk Land.
So Granny waved her wand one final time,
and Jake's runner beans began to grow.

Out of the garden they twisted and
twirled, around the field they swooped
and swirled, then up, up, up they soared into
the sky!

They grew into an *amazing* adventure
playground! "Wow!" gasped everyone.
It was just like Beanstalk Land!

Cheering, everyone bounded off to play. All except Pandora, who was cuddling the little bunny.

"Nibble looks hungry again," she said as he nibbled the end of her sleeve.

Granny looked. "So he does! I'll whizz him up a big, juicy carrot!"

"No!" cried Pandora. Then she giggled. "Well, maybe just a *small* one, Granny. . . ."

The End

Look for more magical
mayhem from Pandora and
her wacky grandmother!